PIC

puzzlehead

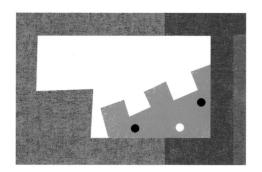

puzzle

head

by James Yang

ginee seo books

Atheneum Books for Young Readers

New York   London   Toronto   Sydney

Atheneum Books for Young Readers
An imprint of Simon & Schuster Children's
Publishing Division
1230 Avenue of the Americas,
New York, New York 10020
Copyright © 2009 by James Yang
Book design by Ann Bobco
The text for this book is set in Filosofia.
The illustrations for this book are digitally rendered.
Manufactured in China
First Edition
2 4 6 8 10 9 7 5 3 1
Library of Congress Cataloging-in-Publication Data
Yang, James, 1960–
Puzzlehead / James Yang. — 1st ed.
p.   cm.
"Ginee Seo books."
Summary: Puzzlehead and his friends go exploring to
find out where they fit in, but Puzzlehead has a hard
time figuring out where he belongs.
ISBN-13: 978-1-4169-0936-1
ISBN-10: 1-4169-0936-2
[1. Friendship—Fiction. 2. Self-acceptance—Fiction.
3. Jigsaw puzzles—Fiction.] I. Title.
PZ7.Y1934Pu 2009
[E]—dc22   2008009664

To the genius who invented recess

Mo, Bob, Sue, and Stevie

were wondering what to do.

"Let's go exploring!" said Puzzlehead.

The best thing about exploring is
you never know what you will find.

"Your legs are not too
    short for this," said Bob.
"I've found the perfect way
    to spin."

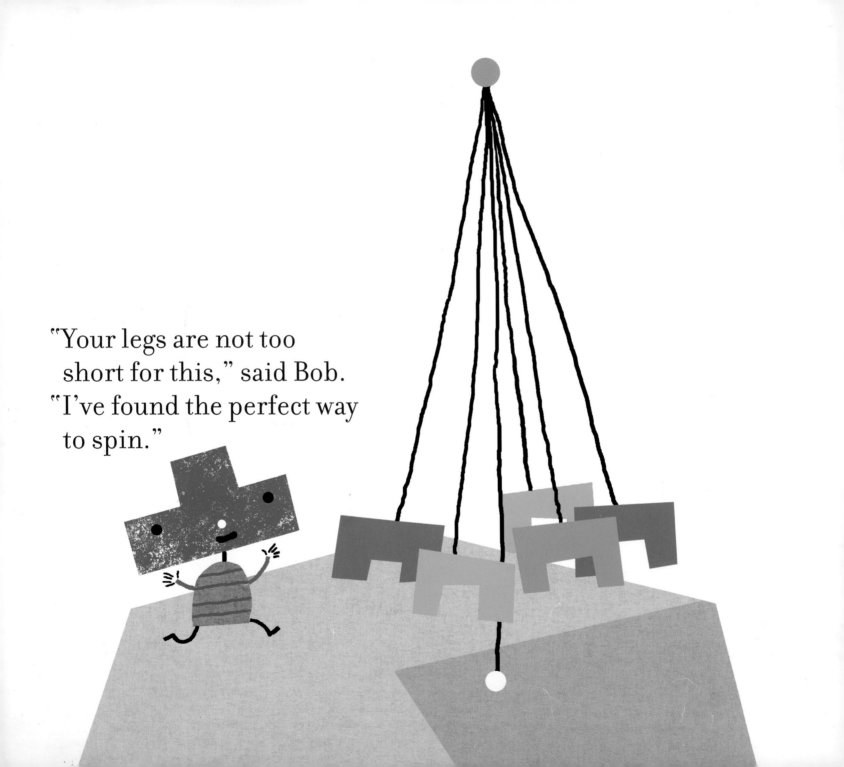

"Come spin with me, Puzzlehead," he said. He went around and around and around.

"That will make me too dizzy," said Puzzlehead. "In fact, I am dizzy just watching you."

"This game will not make you dizzy," said Sue. "This is the perfect game to play with me."

But Puzzlehead did not think so. "I think it will give me a headache," he said.

"Where did Stevie go?"
asked Puzzlehead.
"He was just here."

Stevie tried not to laugh
as Puzzlehead walked by.

Everyone
had found
something
to do.

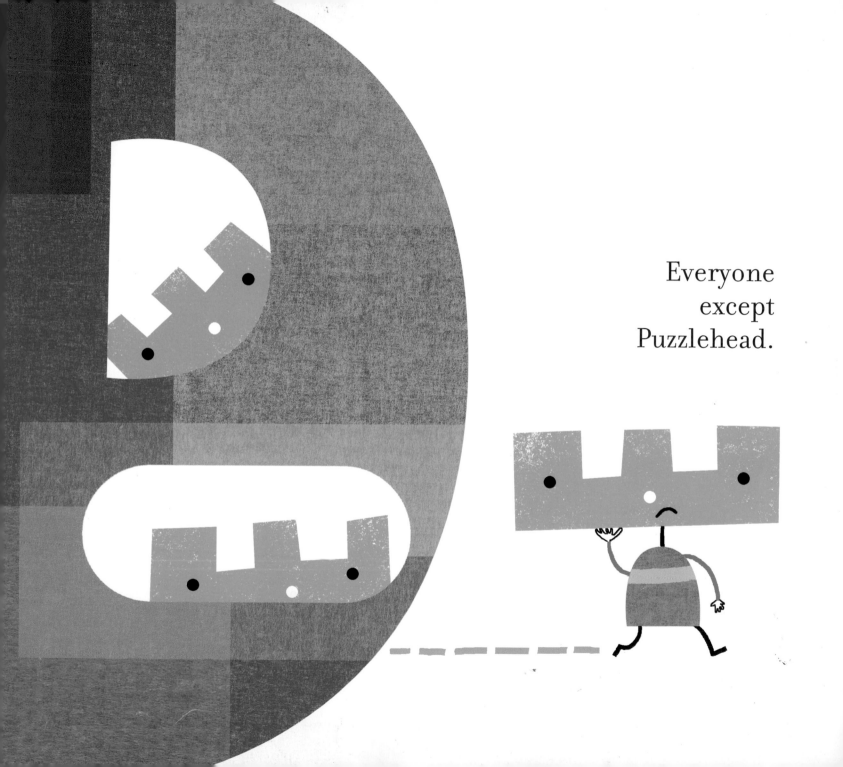

Everyone
except
Puzzlehead.

And then . . .

"Hooray!"

Puzzlehead had found something just right for HIM.
It was a perfect Puzzlehead place.

Puzzlehead wanted to stay there forever.

It was so peaceful and quiet in his Puzzlehead place.

It was VERY peaceful and quiet in his perfect Puzzlehead place.

There was not much to do in his perfect Puzzlehead place.

"Hi, Puzzlehead.
What are you doing?"
asked Sue, Bob, Stevie, and Mo.

"Hi, Sue, Bob, Stevie, and Mo.
I am in my Puzzlehead place.
Isn't it perfect?"

"It's very nice,"
said Sue.

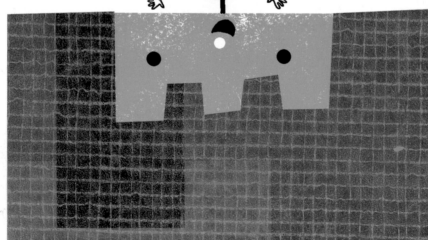

Bob, Stevie, and Mo asked, "But don't you want to play with us?"

"Yes," said Puzzlehead.

There was just one problem.

"Oh, no!"

cried Puzzlehead.

"I'm stuck!"

Sue, Bob, Stevie, and Mo tried to pull Puzzlehead out of his place.

Puzzlehead was still stuck.

They tried harder.
Puzzlehead would
not move.

They pulled and pulled with all their might.

POP!

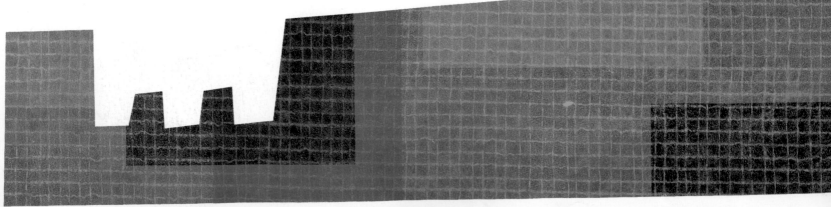

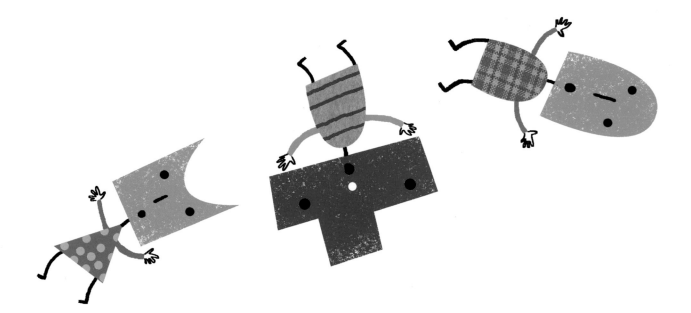
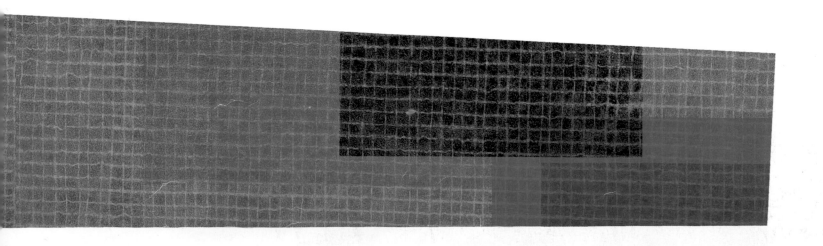

"Help!" yelled Puzzlehead.

"Ow!" yelled Sue.

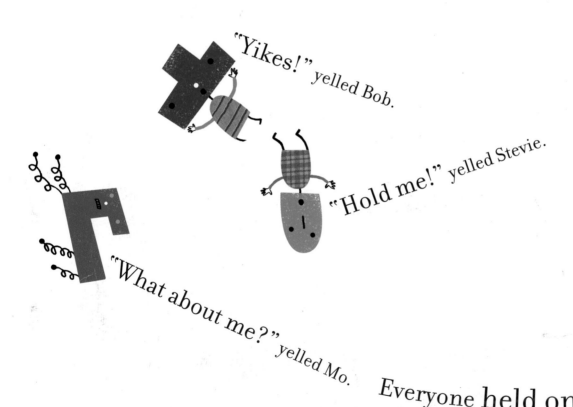

"Yikes!" yelled Bob.

"Hold me!" yelled Stevie.

"What about me?" yelled Mo.   Everyone held one another as they flew up, up, up into the air and then fell down, down, down to the ground.

BLAM!

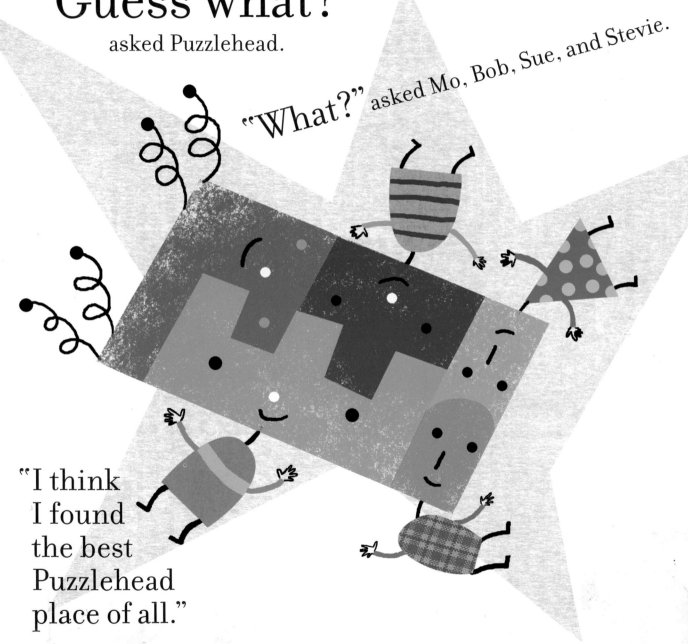

"Guess what?"
asked Puzzlehead.

"What?" asked Mo, Bob, Sue, and Stevie.

"I think
I found
the best
Puzzlehead
place of all."